Neighborhood 3: Requisition on Doom

by Jennifer Haley

A SAMUEL FRENCH ACTING EDITION

SAMUEL FRENCH

FOUNDED 1830

SAMUELFRENCH.COM

ISBN 978-0-573-66323-9   Printed in U.S.A.   #16130

IMPORTANT BILLING AND CREDIT REQUIREMENTS

All producers of *NEIGHBORHOOD 3: REQUISITION OF DOOM must* give credit to the Author of the Play in all programs distributed in connection with performances of the Play, and in all instances in which the title of the Play appears for the purposes of advertising, publicizing or otherwise exploiting the Play and/or a production. The name of the Author *must* appear on a separate line on which no other name appears, immediately following the title and *must* appear in size of type not less than fifty percent of the size of the title type.

In addition the following credit *must* be given in all programs and publicity information distributed in association with this piece:

World premiere of *Neighborhood 3: Requisition of Doom* at
The Human Festival of New American Plays at Actors Theatre of Louisville
New York premiere of *Neighborhood 3: Requisition of Doom*
presented at the Summer Play Festival in association with
The Public Theater

actors theatre of louisville presents
32nd annual Humana Festival of New American Plays
made possible by a generous grant from The Humana Foundation

Neighborhood 3: Requisition of Doom

by **Jennifer Haley**
directed by **Kip Fagan**

March **18 – 30, 2008**

THE CAST

steve, doug, tobias	**John Leonard Thompson**∗
leslie, vicki, barbara, joy	**Kate Hampton**∗
trevor, ryan, jared, zombiekllr14/blake	**Robin Lord Taylor**∗
makaela, kaitlyn, madison, chelsea	**Reyna de Courcy**∗
walkthroughs	**William McNulty**∗

There will be no intermission.

Presented by special arrangement with the Author

Scenic Designer	**Michael B. Raiford**
Costume Designer	**Jessica Ford**
Lighting Designer	**Brian J. Lilienthal**
Sound Designer	**Benjamin Marcum**
Properties Designer	**Doc Manning**
Fight Supervisor	**Lee Look**
Stage Manager	**Bethany Ford**∗
Production Assistant	**Sara Kmack**
Dramaturg	**Amy Wegener**
Casting	**Cindi Rush Casting**

Director underwritten by Tracy and Jonathan Blue

*Member of Actors' Equity Association, the union of professional actors and stage managers of the United States.

Developed with the assistance of New York University's hotINK International Festival of New Play Readings, Seven Devils Playwrights Conference, a project of id Theatre Company at the Alpine Playhouse in McCall, Idaho, and the Brown/Trinity Playwrights Repertory Theatre in Providence, Rhode Island.

The New York premiere of **NEIGHBORHOOD 3: REQUISITION OF DOOM** was presented at the Summer Play Festival in association with The Public Theater. The production was directed by Kerry Whigham with the following cast and crew:

FATHER TYPE . . . . David Aaron Baker
MOTHER TYPE . . . . Sally Wheeler
SON TYPE . . . . Brian Gerard Murray
DAUGHTER TYPE . . . . Reyna de Courcy

Set Designer: Sara Ossana
Lighting Designer: Kathleen Dobbins
Sound Designer: Joanna Lynne Staub
Costume Designer: Hollie Nadel
Fight Choreographer: Jacob Grigolia-Rosenbaum
Blood Specialist: Stephanie Cox-Williams
Assistant Director: Bradley Cherna
Stage Manager: Mei Ling Acevedo
Line Producer: Amanda Berkowitz

players/characters

father type - steve, doug, tobias
mother type - leslie, vicki, barbara, joy
son type - trevor, ryan, jared, zombiekllr14, blake
daughter type - makaela, kaitlyn, madison, chelsea

time/place

right now in the virtual reality
of a video game or suburbia

PRODUCTION NOTES

Most of the play should be staged abstractly, in the netherworld of a video game or modern day suburbia. Realistic elements may be added to Scene 9, so that we feel we are somewhere recognizable, comfortable, and may imagine, for a little while, that none of what's happened previously in the play is real.

A knowledge of MMORPGs, or Massive(ly) Multiplayer Online Role-Playing Games, such as *World of Warcraft*, is helpful in understanding this play.

The language should be spoken as it appears on the page. However, the line breaks represent the briefest of pauses, should be emotionally motivated (not robotic), and sound almost natural. The walkthroughs may be voiceovers or spoken by the actors.

A note on casting: Although the use of four actors is intended to reinforce the notion of of the characters as similarly-styled avatars, larger groups wishing to perform this play may split the roles up between different actors.

For a look at production photos, or for more information about online role playing, avatars, and gamers gone wrong, visit http://www.jennifer-haley.com/neighborhood.html.

Some Scene Notes

1 kitchen
It is fun for the actress playing Makaela to use a whispery, gravelly monster voice on *i'm coming to get you for real.*

2 front yard
There may be a whiff of sexual attraction between Leslie and Steve.

4 pool
Doug is not a calculated sadist; his behavior arises from fear.

5 gameroom
Chelsea is on a Play Station or Xbox. When her team members' headsets go out, she can use her game controller to send text messages to them via the game. Jared logs into the game using a computer.

7 driveway
This is not a case of physical incest.

8 street
Look at the movement of AFK (away from keyboard) characters in World of Warcraft for zombiekllr14.

The Final House
This is an actual episode of CSI.

The violence should be very dramatic, unbelievable, and loud. Perhaps stupidly spurting blood, like in a video game.

One need not be a chamber to be haunted,
One need not be a house;
The brain has corridors surpassing
Material place.

–Emily Dickinson

1 walkthrough

the house you want is third from the left
as you face the cul de sac
all the houses look the same
be careful

move toward the house slowly
you will hear the sound of your
footsteps
in the street
do not walk too fast

as you approach the house
you will see on the sidewalk
a Claw Hammer

pick this up
you will need it later

like all other houses
this house will have a
flesh colored brick façade
and a welcome mat in front of the door

hint: if you kneel down and
take a closer look at this mat
you will see the word
'welcome' becomes
'help me'

enter the house
on your right is a set of
saloon doors
push through these
and enter
the kitchen

1 kitchen

MAKAELA. you want a coke

TREVOR. okay

MAKAELA. shit
we don't have any
my brother
inhaled them

TREVOR. that's okay

MAKAELA. so then i just have stupid stuff
like grape juice
want some
grape juice

TREVOR. okay

MAKAELA. only
he left like an inch
in the bottle

TREVOR. that's okay

MAKAELA. no it's not
i'm going to rip his balls off

TREVOR. i mean
i don't need grape juice

MAKAELA. well nobody needs grape juice
it'd just be nice
otherwise we've got milk
you want some
milk

TREVOR. no thanks

MAKAELA. it's Chocolate Milk

TREVOR. okay

MAKAELA. it's like we're
eleven
again

TREVOR.	that's the last time i had it when i was over here my mom doesn't buy Chocolate Milk
MAKAELA.	your mom
TREVOR.	what
MAKAELA.	doesn't she sell makeup or something
TREVOR.	vitamin shakes
MAKAELA.	what are those
TREVOR.	shakes with vitamins
MAKAELA.	can you e lab or ate
TREVOR.	it's like powder you add water you make a shake you drink it two times a day
MAKAELA.	does it taste good
TREVOR.	no
MAKAELA.	why do you take it
TREVOR.	my mom says it gives you everything you need
MAKAELA.	does it work are you getting everything you need
TREVOR.	...
MAKAELA.	i always see a bunch of cars in front of your place
TREVOR.	she has meetings at the house she gives demonstrations

MAKAELA.   isn't it like a
pyramid scheme

TREVOR.   what's that

MAKAELA.   you know
you get a bunch of people
there are all these levels
everyone tries to get to the next
level
tries to get to the
top
like scientology
or the mafia

TREVOR.   my mom
is not
in the mafia

MAKAELA.   she doesn't know
you're here

TREVOR.   she's gone
this afternoon

MAKAELA.   it's the first time i've seen you
on the bus

TREVOR.   she drives me

MAKAELA.   i'm getting a car soon

TREVOR.   what kind

MAKAELA.   the brand new kind

TREVOR.   but what make and model

MAKAELA.   i don't know
tyler
my brother
just got a hummer
it's actually his second
hummer
he totaled the first one
almost killed someone
so my dad got him another

	i want something that costs the same price as two fucking hummers like maybe a jag
TREVOR.	you think your dad will get you a jag
MAKAELA.	maybe if i act like a giant jerk who's totally circling the drain he'll buy one to try to save me otherwise it'll probably be a toyota
TREVOR.	...
MAKAELA.	...
TREVOR.	still
MAKAELA.	yeah then i could drive you to school
TREVOR.	my mom drives me
MAKAELA.	wouldn't you rather i mean it's high school
TREVOR.	you don't have the car yet so you can't drive me so there's no point in discussing it
MAKAELA.	no point in discussing it okay dad
TREVOR.	just didn't you say your brother has an xbox
MAKAELA.	...
TREVOR.	...
MAKAELA.	do you want a vicodin my brother's a candy man

i know where he
keeps his stash

TREVOR.   won't that
slow my reflexes

MAKAELA.   haven't you
done it before

TREVOR.   no

MAKAELA.   you should ask mummy
for a sip of her
special shake

TREVOR.   she doesn't make
special shakes

MAKAELA.   she doesn't get
that many people over for
vitamins

TREVOR.   look
i didn't come over here to
do drugs
or listen to you insult my mom
i thought we were playing
a game

MAKAELA.   that's the only reason you came over
you barely said hello to me in four years

TREVOR.   so i'm saying
it now

MAKAELA.   yeah cuz i have
an xbox

TREVOR.   i wanted to
it's just
you know

MAKAELA.   what
your mom

TREVOR.   no not my mom

MAKAELA.   she stopped letting you out
cuz you got so cute

TREVOR.	look shut up makaela i stopped coming over cuz you're such a flippin know-it-all i don't have to take this crap i'm leaving
MAKAELA.	we've got Neighborhood 3
TREVOR.	...
MAKAELA.	...
TREVOR.	you've got Neighborhood 3
MAKAELA.	it's tyler's but i know where he hides it
TREVOR.	...
MAKAELA.	...
TREVOR.	okay but my mom doesn't stop me
MAKAELA.	okay
TREVOR.	okay
MAKAELA.	i have to sneak into his room
TREVOR.	i'm dying to play Neighborhood 3
MAKAELA.	ha that sounds like something out of a horror movie like you're about to play this video game and you think it's just a game but actually it's real but these teenagers don't know it but the audience knows it and this one kid's like i'm dying to play and it's like ooooo foreshadowing

TREVOR.   i've been watching cody play

MAKAELA.   so he's your contact

TREVOR.   he's got all the walkthroughs
so you know what to look for
in the game

MAKAELA.   bet cody doesn't have Chocolate Milk
bet that's why you came over here

TREVOR.   he came on to me

MAKAELA.   no
way
cody came on to you

TREVOR.   i think so
he kept saying
how good I was with the joystick
and they're not even called joysticks
anymore

MAKAELA.   i can't believe it
he's so hot
next time i see him
i'm gonna tell him
i'm pretty good
with a joystick

TREVOR.   are you

MAKAELA.   ...

TREVOR.   ...

MAKAELA.   i could be

TREVOR.   well let's turn on the game
and find out

MAKAELA.   wait
are you
what are you

TREVOR.   the game
what are you

MAKAELA.   nothing

i'll set it up and
you can play

TREVOR. you're not going to play

MAKAELA. nah

TREVOR. do some split screen with me

MAKAELA. no

TREVOR. why not

MAKAELA. this game's fucked up
it maps out
your own Neighborhood
how creepy is that

TREVOR. are you kidding
it's sweet
it's the best use of satellite technology
i can think of

MAKAELA. oh now he's excited

TREVOR. how can you not think it's sweet

MAKAELA. there's no point to it

TREVOR. sure there is
you have to keep getting to the next
level
you have to get to the
top

MAKAELA. and then what

TREVOR. you're out
you're free
you've beat everything and nothing can
hurt you anymore

MAKAELA. my brother beats the shit
out of those things
he gets online
and plays with his friends
the sicker the game
they more they like it

he whacks those Zombies
to smithereens
and spends a little too much time with
them
after they're dead

TREVOR. sometimes it's fun
to be sick
sometimes you need a place
to be sick

MAKAELA. that's not the only place
he's sick
you don't know much
about my brother

TREVOR. he plays
at cody's house

MAKAELA. what

TREVOR. tyler
he's almost almost at
the Last Chapter

MAKAELA. have you been
hanging out
with him

TREVOR. they won't let me
play the game
they keep calling me
a noob

MAKAELA. what else
do you do
with them

TREVOR. what do you
mean

MAKAELA. any of that other
sick shit
any of their missions

in the Neighborhood

TREVOR.　　missions

MAKAELA.　　maybe your mom
would want to know about this
would want to know about her
beautiful vitamin shake boy
what if i told
your mom

TREVOR.　　you say a fucking
word to my mom and i'll

MAKAELA.　　what
slice my titties off
like they do the girl Zombies
in the game

TREVOR.　　...

MAKAELA.　　...

TREVOR.　　you're nuts

MAKAELA.　　just leave

TREVOR.　　you're the one
who invited me

MAKAELA.　　i didn't know
you'd got so twisted

TREVOR.　　it's only
a game

MAKAELA.　　oh right trevor
don't tell me
you've never seen it

TREVOR.　　seen what

MAKAELA.　　one of those things
like
reach out

TREVOR.　　what things

MAKAELA.　　in the game

while you're hacking it
reach out with what's left of its
hand
and gurgle
i'm coming
to get you
for real

2 walkthrough

drink the
Chocolate Milk
to replenish your
Sugar Rush

exit the house and
advance down the street
slowly
remember
all action
must appear
unhurried
the goal
during the daytime
is to blend in

two blocks down
on your right
look for the house
with a Garden Gnome
in the front yard

use your Hammer
to break the Gnome
inside you will find a
Pink Post-it Note
with three numbers on it

add this to your inventory
and proceed
up the sidewalk

2 front door

STEVE.   hi there
                hi

LESLIE.   yes

STEVE.   i'm sorry i
                accidentally kicked
                your Garden Gnome

LESLIE.   oh

STEVE.   it's just
                his head
                i've got some
                superglue

LESLIE.   no that's

STEVE.   you might want to keep him
                out back
                i don't think Garden Gnomes are
                acceptable
                to the Neighborhood Association

LESLIE.   are you with
                the Neighborhood Association

STEVE.   no i

LESLIE.   oh i
                thought you were a
                representative
                come to give me another
                warning

STEVE.   no i'm
                from down the street
                i'm

LESLIE.   of course
                halloween

STEVE.   halloween
                yes

i was in
the gorilla suit
until

LESLIE.   yes
i remember

STEVE.   i sometimes get
carried away at
block parties

LESLIE.   well this one was
unseasonably warm

STEVE   ...

LESLIE.   ...

STEVE.   steve

LESLIE.   leslie

STEVE.   you have
twins
right
both of them
were there
the wolfman and
cinderella

LESLIE.   the hunchback and
tinkerbell

STEVE.   tinkerbell
oh right
my daughter was
freddy krueger

LESLIE.   with
the hat

STEVE.   yes

LESLIE.   oh i didn't know
that was a
girl

STEVE.   sometimes neither do we

LESLIE.   ...

STEVE.   uh so
i'm home from the office
early today
i went in the house
and couldn't find my daughter
chelsea
my wife is
taking a break from
the family
so i'm kind of
holding down the fort ha ha
and
well
um

LESLIE.   i'm sorry
but

STEVE.   yeah
it's hard

LESLIE.   no
we're having
a party
for my husband
when he gets home
i'm making
buffalo wings

STEVE.   a party
oh
that's nice
that's really nice
well i won't
take up your time
i just um
let me ask you real quick
have you heard about these
online video games
the kids are playing

LESLIE.   ...

LESLIE.   why do you
ask

STEVE.   my only daughter
chelsea
is hooked on one
Neighborhood
something
i don't know
but when i say
hooked
i guess i'm
putting it mildly
she basically plays this
every waking moment
from the time she gets home from school
to the time she goes to bed
if she goes to bed
we bought her a
high speed gaming computer
for christmas
we thought that would make her
happy
we didn't know
we'd never see her again
she gets online
and plays this character
with other people online
playing characters
some of them
are her friends
but some of them
for all i know
could be pedophiles
they conspire for hours
on that instant message
and conference calls
they run around a Neighborhood

that looks very much like
ours
butchering Zombies
who look a whole lot like
us
but let's see
what am i worried about

i'm worried that
she's not making real friends in the
real world
the way she looks
no one at school will
talk to her
when i was a kid
i made bombs out of firecrackers
and my folks thought i was
possessed
and of course they were
overreacting
and
i've threatened to
remove the computer
but i don't know if it is the computer
or if it's

i'm a
corporate manager
i manage people at all levels
and when they're not up to task i just
fire them
but you know
you can't fire your only kid
even when she comes out of her room
looking like some kind of
monster

LESLIE.　　　...

STEVE.　　　i'm sorry
　　　　　　　of course
　　　　　　　your party

LESLIE.   no let me
come outside
my daughter
madison
plays this game

STEVE.   really

LESLIE.   i can't get her to
come to dinner
we used to think it was
anorexia
until i figured out i had to
set the food down
right in front of her

STEVE.   that's what i do
i pick chelsea up
a burger
everyday
on my way home from work

LESLIE.   i circle back
for the dirty dishes
she screams when i
make her stop for half a minute
to clean drippings
out of the keyboard

STEVE.   her mom and i were dating
by her age
but she's never mentioned
a single boy

LESLIE.   i'd be terrified to see
what kind of date
she'd bring home

STEVE.   she won't allow me
in her room

LESLIE.   she calls me
leslie
she won't call me
mom

STEVE.   what about taking
                the computer away

LESLIE.   she'd just go to
                someone else's house

STEVE.   that's what i thought
                i'd be in our house
                alone

LESLIE.   we'd never see her
                we want to see her
                it's hard enough
                with her father

STEVE.   it's his
                birthday

LESLIE.   no
                no
                not that kind of
                party
                he's a judge
                a federal judge
                he has to decide
                right and wrong all the time
                it's really quite stressful
                i'm hoping it will
                end soon
                i hear her talking to
                the other players
                something about
                the Last Chapter
                they're almost at
                the Last Chapter
                doesn't that sound
                promising

STEVE.   i thought
                your daughter was
                tinkerbell

LESLIE.   it was dark

at the block party
you didn't notice
the hoofprints
on her chest
she went as
tinkerbell bride of satan

STEVE   ...

LESLIE.   ...

STEVE.   i came home
and found her gone
i looked on
her computer
this game is
quite sophisticated
it uses global positioning
to map out the Neighborhood
there's a key for points of
Zombie infiltration
several houses
including mine
and yours
are red

LESLIE.   ...

STEVE.   i want
to talk
to madison

LESLIE.   she's on her
game

STEVE.   she may know
where chelsea is

LESLIE.   i can't
disturb her

STEVE.   we don't know what they're
really up to

LESLIE.   tonight is already
very hard

STEVE.   i don't know anymore
                what's serious
                what if this is
                serious

LESLIE.   i know serious
                i know serious
                you think i don't know
                serious

STEVE.   no i

LESLIE.   they're making me do this tonight
                his friends from work
                this wasn't my idea
                everyone coming over
                to tell him he's drinking
                it's so stupid
                he knows he's drinking
                he'll think this is
                my idea and then
                i don't know
                i don't know
                i don't know anything anymore

STEVE.   i'm sorry

                i guess
                this is not a good night
                here's your
                Gnome

LESLIE.   ...

STEVE   ...

LESLIE.   i liked
                the Gnome
                everyone else in the family
                hated him
                but
                he was always so cheerful
                on the front lawn
                i'd sit down next to him

and put my hands
on his cheeks
when it's warm out
they're warm
when it's cold out
they're cold
the logic
is so appealing
when it's warm out and turns cold
his cheeks are still warm
so you have a history
but only a recent history
just the past hour
instead of the crushing history
of your lifetime
or your country
or hominids

STEVE. i'm sorry i
kicked him
i've got some
superglue

LESLIE. ...

STEVE ...

LESLIE. no

STEVE. no

LESLIE. i think
his time
is up

3 walkthrough

enter the house
you will find yourself in a
living room
with white walls and a
white carpet

turn to your left
proceed up the stairs
and enter the
bedroom

across the room
is a closet
warning: do not enter
this closet
unless you picked up the
Weed Wacker
in Chapter Four

instead
on the nightstand
you will see the
Glass of Red Wine

drink this

when you exit the bedroom
and go back down the stairs
you will notice a pool of
blood
on the carpet

you have just moved through
a secret wormhole
in the Neighborhood
you are now in a house
on the opposite side
of the subdivision

3 living room

VICKI. did you get what you were
looking for

KAITLYN. yes thank you for letting me in
his room

VICKI. hopefully he won't find out
we were in
his room
unless he has some
hidden camera

KAITLYN. i don't remember
a camera

VICKI. i'm kidding
although i wouldn't be surprised
he's always been into
gadgets

KAITLYN. yeah

VICKI. i don't know what he has in there
he keeps it such a big
secret
but we've always pledged
to protect his
privacy

KAITLYN. uh huh

VICKI. well this will be
our
little secret

KAITLYN. um
i should be going
but thank you again
mrs. prichard

VICKI. vicki
it's still vicki
and it's no problem

i'm glad you found
what you were looking for
it's so good so good to see you again

KAITLYN.   it's good to see you
too

VICKI.   we really miss you
around here

KAITLYN.   yeah
me too

VICKI.   my husband and i
thought you were really
good for him

KAITLYN.   thanks
but i should

VICKI.   do you want to sit down
for a minute

KAITLYN.   oh

VICKI.   i could get you a coke
or even a Glass of Wine
i'm having a Glass of Wine
only if you think
your mom wouldn't mind

KAITLYN.   no she lets me
have Wine sometimes
it's just i

VICKI.   i don't expect
tyler home
anytime soon

KAITLYN.   okay
i guess i could
for a minute

VICKI.   great
great
sit down
let me get you

a glass
did you notice
we reupholstered the loveseat

KAITLYN.   it looks nice

VICKI.   thank you
it was not cheap

KAITLYN.   no it looks
nice

VICKI.   i went back and forth on the material
i just couldn't decide between
stripes or oriental
it doesn't seem like a big decision
but it affects the whole room
these things that seem so small
have such enormous consequences
here you go

KAITLYN.   thank you

VICKI.   so
kaitlyn
how's school

KAITLYN.   fine

VICKI.   what electives
are you taking

KAITLYN.   graphic design

VICKI.   really
on the computer

KAITLYN.   oh yeah

VICKI.   wow
they teach you such
great things now
how are the grades
still good

KAITLYN.   i guess

VICKI.   you know

even though
we got him that hummer
tyler's grades took a downturn
when you two split up

KAITLYN.   oh
                  i'm sorry

VICKI.   no
                  no
                  it's not your fault
                  i just think he was
                  upset

KAITLYN.   ...

VICKI.   i mean
                  you were the one
                  to break up
                  with him

KAITLYN.   sort of

VICKI.   that's what
                  he said

KAITLYN.   we weren't
                  hanging out much
                  anyway

VICKI.   but
                  when he wasn't on
                  his computer
                  i thought he was
                  with you

KAITLYN.   i mean
                  sometimes

VICKI.   almost every night of the week

KAITLYN.   no

VICKI.   well where could he
                  have been

KAITLYN.   probably
                  with his friends

VICKI.   you mean the olson boys

KAITLYN.   he's not really
friends with them

VICKI.   those are his
best friends

KAITLYN.   ...

VICKI.   ...

KAITLYN.   ...

VICKI.   it was strange to see his room
i haven't seen it in months
we bought that bed
when he was five years old
one morning i went in
and his feet were poking
off the end
and they were

hairy

i said it was time
for a new bed
but that was when
he sealed off the room
and like i said
i want to give him
a place of his own
to be himself
isn't that good
i'm not the kind of parent
to read her son's diary
if boys really keep diaries
maybe he has a
what is it called
a blog
even if it was online
i wouldn't read it
not that i'm too savvy
with the internet

he's playing that
game now
that takes up
all his time
when he's not out with his
friends
or whoever
he goes out with
i'm just trying to
something's different
do you think
gosh
do you think it's
drugs

KAITLYN.   maybe that's
part of it

VICKI.   he has those
red eyes
but that's just marijuana
right

KAITLYN.   not like
that kind of
red

VICKI.   you mean
something harder
something like
it was on dateline
oxycontin

KAITLYN.   maybe not even
drugs

VICKI.   he has a great imagination
he gets into trouble
with the Neighborhood Association
but so would a saint
i mean
who cares about the stupid golf course
it was strange

to see those posters
on his walls
but all the boys
have posters like that
with skeletons
and Zombies
and blood
right

VICKI.   ...

KAITLYN.   ...

KAITLYN.   i think you should go through his room

VICKI.   ...

KAITLYN.   ...

VICKI.   what do you think
i might find

KAITLYN.   do you remember
that Cat

VICKI.   what Cat

KAITLYN.   the hendersons
Cat

VICKI.   wasn't it
hit by a car

KAITLYN.   you didn't hear
how they found it

VICKI.   how did they
find it

KAITLYN.   it was
still alive
even though

VICKI.   stop

i don't know what
this has to do with
my son
we give him

everything
he needs
this Wine is
too sweet
it's making me
sick
i suppose i do need to let you
get home
i'm so glad you
stopped by
say hello
to your mother
for me
i see her in the
grocery store
all the time
and we keep making plans to
get together
but we just can't seem to
get together
you only live a few blocks over
so i don't know
what it is
but tell her i really will
call her
and we really will
get together

KAITLYN.   okay
thanks for the
Wine
and letting me
in

VICKI.   of course
of course
come back if you need
anything else

what was it
that you needed

KAITLYN.   sorry

VICKI.   from his
                room

KAITLYN.   just something
                of mine
                he took

VICKI.   something
                like
                what

KAITLYN.   it's
                private

VICKI.   oh

KAITLYN.   i mean

VICKI.   no that's
                okay
                of course i
                respect that

KAITLYN.   ...

KAITLYN.   did you know
                this house
                is the mirror opposite
                of mine

VICKI.   ...

KAITLYN.   if you divide the Neighborhood
                along the line of the sewage ditch
                and fold it in half
                my room
                would be right on top of
                his room
                so we'd see each other
                through the ceiling
                which is kind of how
                we got together
                when i needed to escape
                my mom

i could lie in bed
and look through the ceiling
down at him in his bed
looking up through the ceiling
and we just sort of
knew each other

he started playing
that game
it uploads floorplans
from the Neighborhood Association
he showed me a map
of the subdivision
and the wormhole
between our rooms
there are wormholes
all over
the Neighborhood
he said
one of them connects
your imagination
in the game
to what happens
in life
for real
it's not just
the Cat
vicki
i think you should go through his room

VICKI.   his father's
a real estate agent
i quit my job
to be home for him

KAITLYN.   if you don't
look at something
it can kind of
blow up
don't you want to know what's in his

VICKI.   no
                     he needs the right
                     to his own
                     privacy
                     and we give him
                     everything
                     he needs

4 walkthrough

before you are through
back away
from the Cat
do not let the mewing
deter you

leaving it
half alive
will boost your
Ruthless Ratings
which will help you
in future combat

continue down the street
casually
one block up
you will see a house
with a flagstone path
leading to
the back

take this path
to a wooden gate
use your Hammer
to smash the lock
enter the back yard
and proceed to
the pool

4 pool

DOUG.   it's okay son
              things die
              Snickers had a
              good life

RYAN.   ...

DOUG.   we don't really know what happens
              when something dies
              Snickers could be with us
              right here
              right now
              we could even say
              hello Snickers
              you were an awesome cat
              i'm sorry you got hit by that
              hummer
              at least it happened fast
              we should all hope to be
              so lucky

RYAN.   ...

DOUG.   as henry david thoreau said
              i went to the woods
              because i wished to live deliberately
              to front only the
              essential facts of life
              and not
              when i came to die
              discover that i had not lived

RYAN.   Snickers didn't go to the woods

DOUG.   well he went into the bushes a lot

RYAN.   ...

DOUG.   look
              ryan
              we've all been affected
              by the death of Snickers

RYAN.   ...

DOUG.   it reminds us of our own mortality
               and i know that can be scary
               as inderpal bahra said
               we are afraid to live
               but scared to die

RYAN.   ...

DOUG.   death comes to everyone
               think of it as something really democratic
               like our country

RYAN.   or as warren leblanc said
               life is like a video game
               everyone must die

DOUG.   who is warren leblanc

RYAN.   he got caught up in this game called man-
               hunt
               and killed his fourteen-year-old friend
               with a Claw Hammer

DOUG.   ...

RYAN.   ...

DOUG.   that's not quite
               what i mean
               look
               ryan
               we need to do something about this
               crying
               everyone has had a
               good cry over Snickers
               now it's time to dry our eyes
               lift the shades
               and let in the sun
               do you think you can do that

RYAN.   ...

DOUG.   you're not a child anymore
               part of growing up is realizing

there's a lot of pain in this world
and taking responsibility for your life
means you don't let it destroy you
and you don't let your behavior
increase the pain and fear
for everyone else

RYAN.   …

DOUG.   your mother wants to put you
on anti-depressants
do you want to be put
on anti-depressants

RYAN.   um

DOUG.   i didn't think so
we don't need drugs
to repair ourselves
the answer is within us
our personal power
is greater
than we realize
you've always been a good son
we depend on you to keep us in
good spirits
now
we've given you
a break on your chores
since Snickers passed
but i think reinstating them
will help take your mind off things
as henri matisse said
derive happiness in oneself
from a good day's work
so
ryan
you know the grind
clean the filters
skim the leaves
and replace the chlorine tablets
okay

RYAN.   ...

RYAN.   i don't like
               the Barracuda

DOUG.   it helps us
               keep the pool clean

RYAN.   i don't like
               the way it moves

DOUG.   what are you
               ten years old
               it's not as though it's
               alive

RYAN.   maybe not the way we think of
               life

DOUG.   well i guess we have
               two options here
               we could turn it off
               or
               you could practice getting over
               your fear of it
               which would you rather do

RYAN.   ...

DOUG.   which would be the
               brave
               thing to do

RYAN.   ...

DOUG.   look

RYAN.   i just don't want it going
               while i'm cleaning the pool
               is that so
               fucking
               hard

DOUG.   ...

RYAN.   ...

DOUG.   is there something else
               besides Snickers

RYAN.   ...

DOUG.   ...

RYAN.   it's just
               something
               in the Neighborhood

DOUG.   what

RYAN.   i don't know
               i don't think Snickers
               was hit by a hummer

DOUG.   your mom saw it
               pulling around the block

RYAN.   i just don't
               the way Snickers looked
               it just
               didn't look
               like a car
               did that

DOUG.   what did it
               look like

RYAN.   i've been playing this
               game
               at blake's house

DOUG.   we have seen a bit
               less of you

RYAN.   and we
               there's this part with this
               Cat
               and we
               we
               i didn't think
               it was
               real

DOUG.   what was
               real

RYAN.   that
                  it would
                  Snickers
                  dad
                  listen
                  there's something
                  in the Neighborhood
                  something's
                  coming

DOUG.   ...

RYAN.   ...

DOUG.   ...

RYAN.   ...

DOUG.   do you remember
                  what i was saying
                  about personal power
                  being a wonderful thing
                  well it works both ways
                  personal power
                  can do great damage
                  when it's negative
                  you're beginning
                  to remind me
                  of my sister
                  every morning
                  when she woke up
                  you'd hear this
                  wail
                  up above
                  this wail
                  would sound
                  and you'd think
                  here she comes
                  she'd appear
                  at the top of the stairs
                  with her pigtails all twisted
                  her mouth wide open and wet

hair sticking to the mucus on her cheeks
she'd come down the stairs
one pajama foot
after the next
dragging her yellow blanket behind her
plunking down and
down and
closer and
closer
her howls sounding
louder and
louder
god
nothing will scare you more
than your own family

as charles manson said
from the world of darkness
did i loose demons and devils
let me tell you
son
don't you dare
bring something like that
into this house

5 walkthrough

once you've vanquished
the Barracuda
open the filter
behind its mouth
you will find a
Lime Post-it Note
with four numbers on it
add this to your inventory
and exit the back yard

the only way
to escape the Neighborhood
is to enter the
Final House
you must enter the
Final House
before the Neighborhood
is overrun
by Zombies

proceed past the
pocket park
to the house with the
open garage
if you have any available
light weapon slots
turn to the
gas grill
and pick up the
Barbecue Fork

enter the house
through the back of the garage
and find yourself in
the gameroom

5 gameroom

JARED.   come on
                madison
                it's going to start

MADISON.   i'm coming

JARED.   no
                come on
                now

MADISON.   i said
                i'm coming

JARED.   you always say that
                it's never true
                he's on his way home from work
                he'll be here any minute

MADISON.   i'll be right
                there

JARED.   i'm not mom
                don't feed me bullshit
                she went through alot
                to pull this together
                don't you think it's more important
                than your game

MADISON.   we're almost at
                the Final House

JARED.   you worked on
                what you're going to say to him
                didn't you

MADISON.   did you

JARED.   sort of

MADISON.   what are you
                going to say

JARED.   i asked you first

MADISON.   i'll just tell him
                he's totally fucked up
                and he's fucked
                everyone in the family up
                so he should fucking stop
                fucking everyone up
                hey shithole
                get off me
                fucking Zombie
                how about some gut raping
                with my garden spade

JARED.   you're not
                supposed to be
                angry

MADISON.   that's been made
                perfectly clear
                by that douche
                from the facility

JARED.   he's trying to get everyone together
                in the living room
                he told me
                to come get you

MADISON.   well you tell him
                i'm coming

JARED.   ...

MADISON.   ...

JARED.   i'm going to tell dad
                that time he forgot to pick me up
                from baseball practice
                really
                um
                hurt
                i was standing
                on the sidewalk
                and all the other dads
                were picking up their kids

until everyone was
gone
except for me
with my mitt
and it turns out
he was at that bar
in the strip center
he totally
forgot

MADISON.   oh he'll cry
with his big red eyes
and everyone
will feel sorry
for him

JARED.   don't you
feel sorry for him

MADISON.   i'm surrounded by Zombies
where the fuck is my team

JARED.   what if he
can't help it

MADISON.   look i stayed home
didn't i
everyone else
is at cody's house

JARED.   i think you're like him
i think you're
hooked

MADISON.   oh who was sleeping like
two hours a night to play

JARED.   i gave it up

MADISON.   not until the end
you were almost in
the Final House

JARED.   yeah dude
it creeped me out

MADISON. what did

JARED. you're almost there
you'll see

MADISON. i can't get
any closer
hello
chelsea
come in chelsea
where are you guys

JARED. i think we play
to get away from him
like he's trying
to get away from
whatever he's trying to
get away from

MADISON. like us foreclosing

JARED. what do you mean
foreclosing

MADISON. hello
he drank up
all our money

JARED. how do
you know

MADISON. i went in the study
i needed some dough
i went through their records
mom opened a new card
to pay for his fancy rehab
where are they

JARED. madison
would you stop
for a moment
playing that

MADISON. they better not have
ditched me

why does everyone
ditch me

JARED.   for a moment
would you stop
and look at me

MADISON.   no fucking way
they went in
they went in the Final House
they went in without me
now i'll never
get in
i can't do it
on my own

MADISON.   ...

MADISON.   ...

MADISON.   you have to
log in
and help me

JARED.   i'm not playing that
anymore

MADISON.   jared
i need you
you're my twin

JARED.   just stop
and do it
later

MADISON.   i'm not stopping
anymore
i'm not stopping
for him
you've got the computer
it will only take a second

JARED.   there's something
wrong

MADISON.   you've got
                  the circular saw
                  and the lawn darts
                  pleeeeeeeeaaaasee

JARED.   no

MADISON.   pleeeeeeeeeeeeeeaaaaaaaasse

JARED.   no madison

MADISON.   please please please please please please
                  you have to help me or i'll die

JARED.   he'll be home any minute
                  we don't have time

MADISON.   i don't care
                  i hate him
                  i hate him
                  he's messing even this up for me

JARED.   this is nothing
                  don't you care about
                  anything that
                  matters

MADISON.   hold up
                  chelsea's online
                  why isn't she using
                  oh
                  she says her headset is dead

JARED.   besides
                  with the game
                  there's something

MADISON.   weird
                  tyler found a Zombie
                  in the Final House
                  that looked like
                  his mom

JARED.   what'd he do

MADISON.   he pwned her with the Barbecue Fork
                  they're freaking out

chelsea's logging off
she said
don't go in

JARED.   don't go in
where

MADISON.   i'm not going anywhere
cuz i'll get creamed
cuz my team ditched me
shit
mother fucker
die
die
die
die
die
die
die
die
die
die
die

JARED.   listen

MADISON.   what

JARED.   in the Neighborhood

a siren

MADISON.   ...

JARED.   ...

MADISON.   pleeease

JARED.   why don't you put
that energy
into this intervention
if not for him
then for us
maybe it would be
good for us

to
tell the truth
don't you ever want to
shout the truth
out the window
shout
this is the truth
this is the truth
this is the truth

MADISON. fuckin a
you're gonna get us in trouble with
the Neighborhood Association

JARED. i don't care
come and get me
come and get me
Neighborhood Association
come and get me
for telling
the truth

MADISON. you're not even
saying anything
why don't you shout this
every night
on his fifth cocktail
my dad
turns into a Zombie
and basically tells me
what a loser i am
what a loser son i am
so now i
slump
everywhere i go
i'm known at school as
The Hunchback
i still think he's great
way deep down
i'm so glad
the man who deformed me

is taking a month at a spa
to learn he's a
beautiful being
at heart

JARED.   ...

JARED.   ...

JARED.   i don't want to
yell that

MADISON.   yeah cuz it's
the truth

JARED.   ...

MADISON.   ...

JARED.   okay
let me log in

MADISON.   yaaaay

JARED.   have you
figured it out
have you seen
the Final House

MADISON.   no
there's like
twenty Zombies
in my way
if i pop out
they'll see me

JARED.   where are you

MADISON.   in the pocket park
behind the bench

JARED.   i'll distract them

MADISON.   don't die
remember
in the Last Chapter
you can't resurrect

JARED.   you telling me now
              about this game

MADISON.   oh my god
              you're running right out
              in front of them

JARED.   hurry

MADISON.   ...

MADISON.   this isn't a
              suicide mission

JARED.   you wanted to see
              the Final House
              go on
              one block past
              the pocket park
              locate the house on the left

MADISON.   how do you
              remember

JARED.   oh this house
              i could never forget

MADISON.   but

JARED.   go
              go
              go

MADISON.   i'm going

JARED.   a few of them
              are peeling away
              they're coming after
              you

MADISON.   shit
              shit
              i'm almost there
              house on the left
              house on the left
              house on the left
              is

              our house

JARED.   what did i tell you

MADISON.   what happens
                   when you
                   go in

JARED.   i don't know
                   that's where i stopped

MADISON.   i'm on the front porch
                   i'm at the front door

JARED.   oh man
                   did you hear that

MADISON.   ...

JARED.   ...

MADISON.   he's home

6 walkthrough

killing Zombies
will alert the Neighborhood Association
to your presence

as the job
of the Neighborhood Association
is to protect
the Zombies
consider the forces they deploy
to be your
enemy

exit through the garage
proceed down the street
two blocks
and take a
right

in the front yard
of the first house
you will see
a newly-planted crape myrtle tree
with a set of
Hedge Clippers
at its base

move toward
the tree

6 front yard

TOBIAS.	excuse me you're in the way of my Weed Wacker
BARBARA.	you already did this you weed wacked it yesterday
TOBIAS.	i'm weed wacking it again today
BARBARA.	you do it everyday the grass doesn't need it everyday
TOBIAS.	i have to keep it down i have to keep the ground prepared
BARBARA.	i can't hear you could you please turn the Wacker off
TOBIAS.	...
BARBARA.	thank you i'm barbara i'm from next door
TOBIAS.	i've seen you come and go
BARBARA.	you know my son cody
TOBIAS.	i've seen him come and go
BARBARA.	my husband and i just got home cody apparently had some friends over they left the game room a mess a different kind of

mess
you didn't see any of them
come and go
while you were here wacking your
very short grass

TOBIAS.   i just got
started

BARBARA.   but
you don't work
do you
you didn't see them
this afternoon

TOBIAS.   i heard some
screaming

BARBARA.   screaming

TOBIAS.   i think they were playing
some kind of
game

BARBARA.   you mean like
cheering

TOBIAS.   i mean like
screaming

BARBARA.   like they were
excited

TOBIAS.   if by
excited
you mean
frantic
then
yes

BARBARA.   ...

TOBIAS.   ...

BARBARA.   why do you do your lawn
every single day

every day i hear that
buzzing

TOBIAS.   the grass is
unruly
it grows
very fast

BARBARA.   not in a day
not that fast

TOBIAS.   i notice you have
stones

BARBARA.   we filled our yard with stones
so we wouldn't have to mow
i am very sensitive
to noise

TOBIAS.   i'm surprised stones
are allowed
by the Neighborhood Association

BARBARA.   we were one of the first buyers
they wrote our contract
without the grass clause

TOBIAS.   ah the grass clause
you have to have grass
but keep it short
they want it to look like everything
is under control

BARBARA.   what

TOBIAS.   they want it to look like everything
is under control

BARBARA.   i can't hear you
over the sirens

TOBIAS.   everything
is under

control

BARBARA.   they must love you

TOBIAS.   i don't trim my grass
for the Neighborhood Association
i have to keep the ground prepared

BARBARA.   prepared for what

TOBIAS.   ...

BARBARA.   you don't work
do you

TOBIAS.   i stopped finding it
important
i stopped finding alot of things
important

BARBARA.   you did this
today
to your house
why are the
windows boarded

TOBIAS.   protection

BARBARA.   what are we expecting
a hurricane

TOBIAS.   have you looked at
your son's game

BARBARA.   how do you know about

TOBIAS.   it's quite popular
playing with
real people

BARBARA.   i know
some of the people
he plays with
but some of them
i don't
it could be someone next door
or it could be
a pedophile

TOBIAS.   or both

BARBARA.   what do you mean

TOBIAS.   what do you mean

BARBARA.   ...

TOBIAS.   ...

BARBARA.   you don't have children
do you

TOBIAS.   we had a hard time
we took some drugs
we got pregnant with triplets
three girls
dead in the womb
at seven months
we buried them in the yard
under the crape myrtle tree

BARBARA.   isn't that
illegal

TOBIAS.   no
it's our belief
they were
Ballerinas
they died floating in a
pas de trois
at night they come out
and float through the yard
i cut the grass for their glisades
they move on to your place
to practice their grand jetés
you wake up and hear
their pointe shoes
on your stones

BARBARA.   i wake up
and hear that
clacking

TOBIAS.   we moved here
to raise children
and then i realized

this Neighborhood
in trying so hard to
deny fear
actually magnifies it
i could feel it
warping them
in the womb
if they'd been born
it would have warped them
into something
unthinkable
instead
they dance
for the Last Chapter

BARBARA.   the Last Chapter
that's something from
cody's game

TOBIAS.   it was hard
getting it out of him

BARBARA.   getting it out
i thought you hadn't
seen him

TOBIAS.   not today
last night

BARBARA.   last night

TOBIAS.   i caught him in
my yard
he was making
a mess

BARBARA.   what kind of
mess

TOBIAS.   a different kind of
mess

BARBARA.   you have to
tell me
i'm his

mom

TOBIAS.   we believe imagination
creates reality
if you fear something
it will manifest
if you don't face it
it will kill you
are you sure you're ready to
face it

BARBARA.   his father's out
looking for him
his father is
an angry man
if you're not telling us
something we need to know

TOBIAS.   are you sure you're ready to
face it
yes or no

BARBARA.   i'm not playing
this game
with you

TOBIAS.   then if you'll
excuse me

BARBARA.   don't you dare
turn that on

TOBIAS.   are you
threatening me

BARBARA.   yes

TOBIAS.   ...

BARBARA.   yes

TOBIAS.   cody said
in the Final House
there's a wormhole
once you go in
you take your family with you

they appear to you as
Zombies
and finally you can
kill them
without
remorse

BARBARA.   ...

TOBIAS.   ...

BARBARA.   do you know what the neighbors
say about you
they say you killed those girls
you killed them and
buried them in the yard
because you were afraid
they were going to be
monsters

TOBIAS.   monster
who do you think
is the monster

i'll leave out these
Hedge Clippers
if you see
your son
don't hesitate

7 walkthrough

you may pick up the
Hedge Clippers
if you have a proficiency
in garden tools

proceed toward a street sign
that reads 'dead end'
turn left into
the cul de sac

as night
begins
to fall
you may engage the
Run Really Fast Function

your Stealth Talent
increases by
three
Zombie Olfactory Skill
increases by
twelve

turn to the first house
on your right
you will see the
Cell Phone
in the driveway

pick this up
and move toward
the house

7 driveway

STEVE.	there you are i've been looking all over for you
CHELSEA.	not now steve
STEVE.	don't not now steve me chelsea get back inside the house
CHELSEA.	i'm not staying i have to check on my friend
STEVE.	what friend
CHELSEA.	you don't know her
STEVE.	it's too late where have you been all afternoon
CHELSEA.	i was at someone's house
STEVE.	whose house
CHELSEA.	you come home every night in the dark what do you care
STEVE.	i came home early to spend some time with you only to find you gone
CHELSEA.	i have to check on my friend
STEVE.	even when you're here all i see

is you at the computer
with your big bag of cheetos
well that's about to
end

CHELSEA.   you have no idea
what's going on
i don't need
your permission

STEVE.   why don't you
just call her

CHELSEA.   i can't find
my Cell Phone

STEVE.   that's because i have your Cell Phone

CHELSEA.   ...

STEVE   ...

CHELSEA.   give it to me

STEVE.   is this what you came home to look for
it was on the kitchen counter
'lot of interesting stuff here

CHELSEA.   what are you
talking about

STEVE.   fascinating
photo gallery

CHELSEA.   you looked through my
pictures

STEVE.   only
a few
i saw
enough
your dad
may be
a lot of things
but one thing he's not
is a pervert
who are these for

you got a
boyfriend
you're not
telling me

CHELSEA. yeah
a boyfriend
how fucking
quaint

STEVE. your mouth
when did you get so
filthy

CHELSEA. my friend's in
trouble
give me
my Phone

STEVE. your Phone
who do you think
paid for
your Phone
this is a
market economy
i've paid for
this house
this Phone
this driveway
you're standing in
right now
i got the money
to pay for it
because i
work
i have something of
value
what do you have of
value

CHELSEA. i am a level 90 gothic cheerleader
with a plus 12 proficiency

          in the Golf Club
          i suggest
          you give me
          my Phone

STEVE.   my god
          i let you do
          whatever you wanted
          after your mother left
          i've given you
          everything
          why would you take these
          pictures
          why chelsea
          tell me
          why
          and i'll give you
          your Phone

CHELSEA.   currency

STEVE.   you mean money
          i give you

CHELSEA.   in the game
          we have our own
          currency
          i upload
          photos
          to other
          players
          in exchange for
          food
          armor
          weapons
          i know all about
          the market economy
          i know
          what i have
          of value

STEVE   ...

CHELSEA.   ...

STEVE.   get inside

CHELSEA.   you said
you'd give me
my Phone

STEVE.   i've done something
wrong
i can no longer
trust you

CHELSEA.   i can't
trust you
you said
you'd give me

STEVE.   this is not
a debate
this is
an order

CHELSEA.   you don't fucking
understand
there's something
at madison's
house

STEVE.   what did you say to me

CHELSEA.   there's something
at madison's
house

STEVE.   you're lucky
i can't hear you
young lady
over all the
sirens
what's up with
the sirens
what's going on
in the Neighborhood

CHELSEA.   oh my god
go inside
and lock
the door

STEVE.   what

CHELSEA.   give me
my phone
and get
inside

STEVE.   you're the one
who's going
inside

CHELSEA.   dad
listen
we were all playing
at cody's
we went in
the Final House
tyler found a
Zombie
that looked like
his mom
he stuck her through the eyes
with the Barbecue Fork
freaked out
ran home
and called us
screaming
get out of
cody's house
he screamed
cody's father
is after him
his house is covered in
yellow tape
there are sirens and
swat teams

from the Neighborhood Association
i'm trying to
get to madison
to tell her not to
go in
maybe she can help us
if she doesn't
go in

STEVE.   stop it
right now
something is
really wrong with you
are you on
drugs

CHELSEA.   keep the phone
i'll go myself

STEVE.   you're not going
anywhere

CHELSEA.   let go
of me

STEVE.   i don't know
why i didn't
see this
why i didn't
see you

CHELSEA.   let go

STEVE.   maybe i never wanted to
look
and this is what happens
when you don't
look
your family becomes
something you don't
recognize

CHELSEA.   i'm going to scream

STEVE.   your mouth

a wound
your eyes
a ghoul
and those pictures
you didn't used to be like this
my daughter
you used to be so pretty

CHELSEA.   ...

CHELSEA..   ...

STEVE.   i'm sorry
don't cry
i'm sorry
i'm a
monster

CHELSEA.   ...

CHELSEA.   ...

STEVE.   why are you
looking at me
like that

CHELSEA.   ...

STEVE.   where did you get that
Golf Club

CHELSEA.   ...

STEVE.   chelsea
wait
please
no

8 walkthrough

remove the
Pink and Lime Post-it Notes
from your inventory

the numbers on
the Notes
combine to form
a phone number

using the
Cell Phone
text the words
Final House
to this number

you will receive a
return text
that contains your
instructions

as darkness falls
for good
you must use the
streetlights
to track the
Zombies
make sure you have the
Flashlight

and follow your instructions
to the Final House

8 street

ZOMBIEKLLR14. holy shit man
                   WTF

BARBARA.   don't kill me
                   don't kill me

ZOMBIEKLLR14. what

BARBARA.   i'm sorry i
                   knocked you down

ZOMBIEKLLR14. are you a player

BARBARA.   please don't kill me
                   i'm trying to find
                   my son

ZOMBIEKLLR14. i can't kill you
                   if you're a player
                   i'll lose points

BARBARA.   i'm a player
                   i'm a player

ZOMBIEKLLR14. then get down
                   they're alerted
                   to movement

BARBARA.   who are

ZOMBIEKLLR14. ...

BARBARA.   ...

ZOMBIEKLLR14. are you sure
                   you're a player

BARBARA.   i
                   my name is
                   barbara

ZOMBIEKLLR14. barbara
                   your screen name is
                   barbara
                   LOL

BARBARA.   who are you

ZOMBIEKLLR14.   Zombiekllr14

BARBARA.   are you with
the Neighborhood Association

ZOMBIEKLLR14.   do i look like i'm with
the NA

BARBARA.   they're sending out
swat teams
you're wearing all that
armor

ZOMBIEKLLR14.   if i were with
the NA
you'd already be
dead
i'm looking for
the Final House

BARBARA.   no
the Final House
my son
i think
went in
all the sirens
all the houses with
yellow tape
no one will tell me
what's going on
my husband and i
are looking for him
he has to be here
somewhere

ZOMBIEKLLR14.   WTF
get down

BARBARA.   WTF

ZOMBIEKLLR14.   what the fuck
stay out of the
streetlight

i don't know how you got to the
Last Chapter
noob
but you better not give me away

BARBARA.   the Last Chapter
what is it with
the Last Chapter

ZOMBIEKLLR14.   you're really
pretty
you look like
my friend's mom
i always thought
she was hot
where'd you get
that avatar

BARBARA.   avatar
you sound like
my son

ZOMBIEKLLR14.   you have a son
IRL

BARBARA.   IRL

ZOMBIEKLLR14.   in real life
are you like
old

BARBARA.   what was that
in the streetlight

ZOMBIEKLLR14.   the streetlights
are how we
keep track of them

BARBARA.   track of what

ZOMBIEKLLR14.   shit
there's like
fifty
heading this way

BARBARA.   fifty of what
how do you know

ZOMBIEKLLR14. on my headset
one of my team members
told me
aren't you on
a team

BARBARA. i mean
my husband
my son

ZOMBIEKLLR14. come on
keep down
if i have to kill one
we're in trouble

BARBARA. what
have you
been killing
what's that
in your hand
a Hammer
oh my god
it's slimy

ZOMBIEKLLR14. where's your
weapon

BARBARA. i don't have a
weapon

ZOMBIEKLLR14. how'd you get
this far

BARBARA. my neighbor
tried to give me
Hedge Clippers

ZOMBIEKLLR14. oh wow
you've got the Hedge Clippers

BARBARA. no
i didn't take them

ZOMBIEKLLR14. dude
what's wrong with you

BARBARA.   i thought he was
crazy

ZOMBIEKLLR14. you're the one
who's crazy
get the fuck
away from me

BARBARA.   wait
where are you
going

ZOMBIEKLLR14. there are fifty of them
hot on our tracks
you're going
to give me
away

BARBARA.   oh my god

ZOMBIEKLLR14. OMG

BARBARA.   oh my god

ZOMBIEKLLR14. it's OMG

BARBARA.   OMG
fifty of what

ZOMBIEKLLR14. fifty Zombies

BARBARA.   ...

BARBARA.   i don't believe in
Zombies

ZOMBIEKLLR14. AFK

BARBARA.   AFK

ZOMBIEKLLR14. away from keyboard

BARBARA.   keyboard
what are you
talking about
what the hell are you
talking about
i don't believe in
Zombies

  do you hear me
  i don't believe in

  what was that
  was that what i
  think it
  was that
  did you see that
  hey
  did you see that
  hello
  what's wrong with you
  you said there were
  Zombies
  so why don't you
  do something
  do something
  do something

ZOMBIEKLLR14. i'm back
  sorry
  i had to shut my window
  there was some woman outside screaming
  now what was i doing
  oh yeah
  ditching you

BARBARA. wait
  i saw something

ZOMBIEKLLR14. where

BARBARA. over there
  in the streetlight

ZOMBIEKLLR14. that's the only way
  to see them coming

BARBARA. ...

ZOMBIEKLLR14. ...

BARBARA. ...

ZOMBIEKLLR14. WTF

BARBARA.   what happened to
               the streetlights

ZOMBIEKLLR14. the NA must have
               turned them off

BARBARA.   it's so dark
               i can't see
               anything

ZOMBIEKLLR14. where the fuck is my team
               come in
               KneelBeforeMe
               are the lights out
               where you are

BARBARA.   my god
               where am i

ZOMBIEKLLR14. KneelBeforeMe
               where are you man

BARBARA.   where am i where am i

ZOMBIEKLLR14. you better
               come in
               you've got
               the Flashlight

BARBARA.   i have a
               Flashlight

ZOMBIEKLLR14. you have the
               Flashlight
               f'n a
               turn it on

BARBARA.   ...

BARBARA.   Last Chapter
               Final House
               Zombies
               OMG
               am i in
               cody's game

ZOMBIEKLLR14. ...

BARBARA.   ...

ZOMBIEKLLR14. you know
                   cody

BARBARA.   cody
                     is my
                     son

ZOMBIEKLLR14. mrs. whitestone
                   it's me
                   blake

BARBARA.   blake
                     blake
                     you're
                     seven feet tall

ZOMBIEKLLR14. dude
                   i thought i recognized you
                   how'd cody find an avatar
                   that looks so much like you

BARBARA.   where is he

ZOMBIEKLLR14. last time i heard
                   he had a fuckload
                   i mean buttload of Zombies after him
                   one of them looked like
                   his dad

BARBARA.   OMG
                     i've got to
                     find them

ZOMBIEKLLR14. where are you going
                   with that
                   Flashlight

BARBARA.   cody's in
                     trouble

ZOMBIEKLLR14. i need you
                   i need you to get to the
                   Final House

BARBARA.   no

don't go in the
Final House

ZOMBIEKLLR14. that's the only way
out of the Neighborhood
i need you to follow me
and keep the light
in front of us

BARBARA. i can find him
on my own

ZOMBIEKLLR14. i'm sorry to say this mrs. whitestone
but i will waste you
and you know
if you die
in the Last Chapter
you can no longer
resurrect

BARBARA. ...

ZOMBIEKLLR14. over there
up one block
let's go

BARBARA. ...

ZOMBIEKLLR14. ...

BARBARA. ewgh
something
dripped
on me

ZOMBIEKLLR14. come on
come on

BARBARA. it felt
warm

ZOMBIEKLLR14. felt
that's some imagination you got there
mrs. whitestone

BARBARA. what is up there
in that tree

ZOMBIEKLLR14. don't worry
it's dead

BARBARA. but it looks like
someone i

ZOMBIEKLLR14. just keep
the light
in front of us

BARBARA. ...

ZOMBIEKLLR14. ...

BARBARA. did you hear that

ZOMBIEKLLR14. yeah
that was creepy
shine the light
over there

BARBARA. OMG

ZOMBIEKLLR14. WTF
it looks like

BARBARA. Ballerinas

ZOMBIEKLLR14. what are Ballerinas
doing in the game

BARBARA. don't you get it
Zombie Killer
this isn't

ZOMBIEKLLR14. holy shit
they found it
we're at the
Final House

BARBARA. it's
my house

ZOMBIEKLLR14. it's
my house

BARBARA. cody
i wonder if
what's that on
the porch

ZOMBIEKLLR14. careful

BARBARA.   Post-it Notes
                  they're covered in

ZOMBIEKLLR14. yeah
                  the blood effects are
                  killer

BARBARA.   are these
                  cody's
                  where is

ZOMBIEKLLR14. i don't know
                  mrs. whitestone
                  he may not
                  resurrect

BARBARA.   what do you mean

ZOMBIEKLLR14. my teammate
                  just told me
                  that Zombie that was after him
                  got him

BARBARA.   i don't
                  no
                  i don't
                  no
                  there must be

ZOMBIEKLLR14. when my team gets here
                  we're going in

BARBARA.   no
                  no
                  don't
                  go in

ZOMBIEKLLR14. that's the only way
                  out of the Neighborhood

BARBARA.   that is not
                  the only way
                  get up
                  from your computer

get up
from your computer
and go talk
to your mom

ZOMBIEKLLR14. i don't talk
to my mom

BARBARA. tell her
barbara sent you
she knows me
from when you and cody
were boys

ZOMBIEKLLR14. she doesn't
listen to me
crap
here she comes

BARBARA. tell her
to contact
my neighbor

ZOMBIEKLLR14. right when i'm
about to
go in

BARBARA. no
do not
go in
maybe
it's not
too late
if some of you
don't
go in
maybe
oh god
cody

ZOMBIEKLLR14. i can't play with her
over my shoulder
fuck
AFK

BARBARA.   wait
blake
blake
tell her
to listen you
talk
to your mom
talk
to each other
oh god
cody
we thought
when we moved here
we were moving
up
but all the Neighborhoods
are mirror images
all the Neighborhoods
fold onto each other
don't go in
the Final House
there are no levels
there's no moving up
there's no
getting
out

9 the final house

(A teenage boy sits at a computer. Light from the monitor shines on his face. He wears a headset and alternately types on the computer keyboard and maneuvers a fancy mouse with a giant tracking ball. Clothes are strewn about his room. Fast food wrappers litter his desk.)

BLAKE. I'm here. *(pause)* At the final house. *(pause)* In the bushes by the front door. *(pause)* Well hurry up. *(pause)* My Cologne du Corpse is wearing off. They're gonna smell me. *(pause)* Please just get your ass over here.

(The door to the bedroom opens. A woman in a fuzzy bathrobe stands in the hall light, clutching a fast food bag.)

JOY. Honey? *(pause)* Are you still on your game? *(pause)* I microwaved your burger since you were too busy to eat it earlier. Do you want it now?

(He ignores her. She is used to it.)

I'm watching a little CSI. I love how that forensic team figures everything out in the end. This episode is about a dwarf – I mean little person – who murders another little person because he's about to marry his daughter – who is normal - I mean, a person of average height. He wants his daughter to marry another person of average height so she'll have a normal family. I mean, everyone wants a normal family. So he murders the little fiancee by hanging him. They even show the vertebrae going snap snap snap. At least, that's what I think was happening. You know I cover my eyes for the gory part. It's too, um, real. *(She hears something downstairs, turns her head for a moment to listen, then turns back to* **BLAKE***.)* I know you're busy, but, it's a little lonely downstairs…don't you want to come sit on the couch with me and watch?

(He ignores her.)

Well. I offered.

(She drops the bag inside the room and closes the door.)

BLAKE. There you are, man! I was getting lonely. *(pause)* Yeah, I'm ready. In a minute. Calm down. Don't you think, um… *(As he talks he gets up from the computer, retrieves the burger, comes back to the computer.)* Don't you think we should wait for the rest of the team? *(pause)* Yeah I know we can, it's just – I have to check my armor one more time. *(pause)* And refill my Sugar Rush. *(pause)* And um…hey, get off the porch, get back in the bushes, I'm not ready yet! *(pause)* I am NOT stalling – !

(door opens)

JOY. Honey? I thought I heard something by the front door. It sounded. Strange. I don't know, maybe I'm imagining things. You aren't – up to anything – are you? You can – tell me – if you are. I promise I won't – freak out. I'd really actually prefer some advance notice to one of those phone calls. Why don't you come downstairs, I'll make some popcorn, we can – talk – and maybe you could listen to this noise and see if you think it sounds strange. Like something coming through the walls. I never used to feel that way about this place. But now. It's like that movie. Maybe our house is built on an indian burial ground. Maybe the neighborhood. Maybe the whole country. Oh now listen to me – being morbid – I must need another – *(She stops herself.)* It's just that thing by the front door. You wouldn't know anything about it, would you? *(pause)* Hey. I'm talking to you. Look at me when I talk to you!

*(**BLAKE** turns his head the tiniest degree possible. Pause.)*

No, of course you wouldn't. Why don't you get ready for bed. I'll bring you something to help you sleep.

(She closes the door.)

BLAKE. Fuck, she makes me insane. *(pause)* No, I'm not ready yet. *(He eats his burger, talking through the food.)* It's not about being a pussy you fucking douche – listen – there was this woman. *(pause)* I wish – no – in the game. I couldn't tell if she was a Zombie or a player. She looked like Cody's mom and kept asking if I'd seen him. *(pause)* Yeah, I thought at first it was Cody being a total weirdo, but. Something was off. She kept saying, don't go in. *(pause)* I know it's lame, but – *(pause)* Look, shut up – I took care of it! That's her on the sidewalk. I bashed her head in.

(Door opens.)

JOY. Blake, I'm sure of it. There's something out there. You're the man of the house now – you should come take a look. It's not just the noise, I saw – a shadow. In the porch light. Coming. To the front door. Hey! Are you listening to me? I am asking you a favor! It's the least you can do after everything I do for you. I cook your meals. I wash your clothes. I make sure you don't shrivel up and – die – behind that computer. The computer that was *bought* for you. And can you be bothered to do a single thing for me? *(pause)* You! I'm talking to you! I'm not just some drudge who does all your shit work! Look at me!

BLAKE. *(Without turning around.)* What.

JOY. What?

BLAKE. I said what.

JOY. Is that all you have to say?

BLAKE. What do you want me to say, Joy?

JOY. Don't call me that!

BLAKE. It's your name.

JOY. I have told you not to call me that! I have told you and told you, but you don't listen to me! You don't listen to a thing I say! And I have done – everything for you! Well let me tell you, buster, things are going to change around here. Nothing's free in this world, and it's time for you to earn your keep. I'm making a list of after school chores and setting limits on your game time. Starting now. Off the computer in five minutes!

(She closes the door. **BLAKE** *straightens.)*

BLAKE. Grrrw, I just got the things-are-gonna-change-around-here speech. But nothing ever does. So fuck it – let's go in. *(pause)* Get up here and cover me. *(pause)* I'm trying the front door…oh weird, weird… it's opening on it's own. *(pause)* I can't see anything inside. *(pause)* You ready? *(pause)* Okay. *(pause)* I'm in, I'm in! *(pause)* I'm behind the sofa come on. *(pause)* Shit I saw something move. *(pause)* In the light of the television. *(pause)* I don't know – just get up the stairs – it's in the bedroom at the top. Bedroom at the top. *(pause)* Wait, don't open the door yet. *(pause)* Do you hear that? *(pause)* Fuck, my heart is pounding. *(pause)* Okay, ready man. *(pause)* Opening the door…I'm… opening the door . . .

(door opens)

JOY. Honey?

BLAKE. Not now!

JOY. I did it. I looked.

BLAKE. You said I have five minutes!

JOY. I didn't have a choice – the front door just – opened.

BLAKE. Get the fuck outta my room!

JOY. Do you remember Barbara, Cody's mom?

(Pause. For the first time, **BLAKE** *turns to look at her.)*

BLAKE. What about her?

JOY. She's on the sidewalk. With half her head gone.

*(***BLAKE** *stares at her in disbelief. Then he whirls back to the computer and jabs at the keyboard.)*

BLAKE. Get out. Get out of the room get out of the house. Get out get out get out get out get out get out fuck the front door is locked.

JOY. I locked the front door.

BLAKE. Are you there man? We're in trouble!

JOY. All night I've heard sirens.

BLAKE. I'm unarmed. I dropped my hammer somewhere on the stairs.

JOY. Is this what you're looking for? I found it on the stairs.

(**BLAKE** *turns around to look.* **JOY** *is holding a bloody claw hammer.*)

BLAKE. Give that to me.

JOY. Does it belong to you?

BLAKE. Look, Joy –

JOY. Don't call me that! Just the fact that you're capable of calling me that…What happened to Barbara?

BLAKE. You tell me.

JOY. No, you tell me. You never tell me anything anymore.

BLAKE. You never ask.

JOY. I try all the time to talk to you.

BLAKE. You don't really want to know.

JOY. You never even look at me anymore.

BLAKE. I'm looking at you now.

JOY. I don't recognize you.

BLAKE. I'm your son. Give me the hammer.

JOY. I have tried to talk to you! I have tried! I want to hear you say, I know you've tried.

BLAKE. Easy, Joy.

JOY. DON'T CALL ME –

BLAKE. OKAY! You've tried.

JOY. Say it like you believe it. Say it like it's the truth.

BLAKE. I. Believe. You've –

JOY. NO. You don't believe me. You don't even see me. You don't see anything outside of your game. You don't see anything that's real!

(*JOY realizes* BLAKE *is cowering from her. She sags.*)

JOY. I'm sorry. (*pause*) It's so good…to see you, son. It's so good…to see your face.

(*Touched,* BLAKE *nods. This is their only moment.*)

I just want to…I just want…the two of us…It's not too late, is it? It's not too late?

(BLAKE *shakes his head.*)

I'm so sorry. So so so so so so so so so –

(*She rushes towards him, arms raised.* BLAKE, *suddenly terror-stricken, wrenches the hammer from her hand and, through her screams, beats her to death.*)

10 bedroom

(**BLAKE** *shoves himself away from the computer. Shivering, he looks around the empty room.*)

BLAKE. Mom?

End

OTHER TITLES AVAILABLE FROM SAMUEL FRENCH

DANGER- GIRLS WORKING
James Reach

Mystery Comedy / 11f / Unit Set

At a New York girl's boarding house, there is a newspaper woman who wants to write a novel, a wise cracking shop girl, the serious music student, a faded actress, a girl looking for romance, the kid who wants to crash Broadway and other boarders. The landlady, is the proud custodian of the "McCarthy Collection," a group of perfect uncut diamonds. When it disappears from the safe, the newspaper woman is given two hours to solve the case before the police are called. Suspicion is cleverly shifted from one to the other of the girls and there's a very surprising solution.